MY FAVORITE DOG

CHIHUAHUAS

by Diane Bailey
Dog Expert: Beth Adelman, MS
Former editor, *American Kennel Club Gazette*

Kaleidoscope
Minneapolis, MN

The Quest for Discovery Never Ends

This edition first published in 2021 by Kaleidoscope Publishing, Inc.

*For information regarding permission, write to Kaleidoscope Publishing, Inc.
6012 Blue Circle Drive
Minnetonka, MN 55343*

*Library of Congress Control Number
2020936227*

*ISBN
978-1-64519-438-5 (library bound)
978-1-64519-450-7 (ebook)*

Printed in the United States of America.

FIND ME IF YOU CAN!

Bigfoot lurks within one of the images in this book. It's up to you to find him!

TABLE OF CONTENTS

Introduction

Here Comes a Chihuahua!

Ali has been asking for a dog for a long time. His parents finally said yes! They drive to the animal shelter early in the morning. Ali is excited to pick out his new friend. "Remember," the shelter worker says, "the dog has to pick you, too."

Ali walks through the **kennels**. Who will pick him?

Yip! Yip!

Ali kneels down beside one kennel. A Chihuahua is curled up on a blanket in the corner. She perks her ears forward. Then she trots over and sticks her tiny head up against the kennel bars. *Yip?* This time it sounds like a question. Ali knows the answer!

"I think I just got picked!" Ali laughs. He glances at the name tag on the kennel. "Let's take Pepper home."

FUN FACT

The Chihuahua is named for a state in Mexico that is just south of Texas.

Chapter 1
The Story of Chihuahuas

Chihuahuas most likely come from another type of dog called the Techichi. These dogs were kept by the Toltec people. They lived more than 1,000 years ago in what is now Mexico. The Techichi were larger than modern Chihuahuas, but they looked a lot alike. The Toltec

This drawing shows what a Techichi might have looked like (far right).

took good care of their Techichi. They believed their dogs had special powers, such as being able to see into the future and cure sick people.

Spanish explorers started arriving in Mexico in the 1500s. Historians think they brought a kind of small, hairless dog with them. It originally came from China. These dogs were bred with the Techichi. The result was the Chihuahua. Chihuahuas came to the United States by about 1850. Now they are one of the country's most popular dogs.

FUN FACT

Dog people call Chihuahuas "Chis" for short.

Dog breeds belong to different groups. Chihuahuas are part of the Toy Group. Sometimes the group is called Companion Dogs. Whatever name is used, these groups include the smallest breeds of dogs. Chihuahuas were not bred to be working dogs who did a special job. They were meant to keep their humans company.

ON THE PROWL

Despite their small size, Chihuahuas can be fearless hunters. They are good at tracking down mice, rats, and even squirrels. In parts of Mexico, some people train their Chihuahuas to hunt vermin.

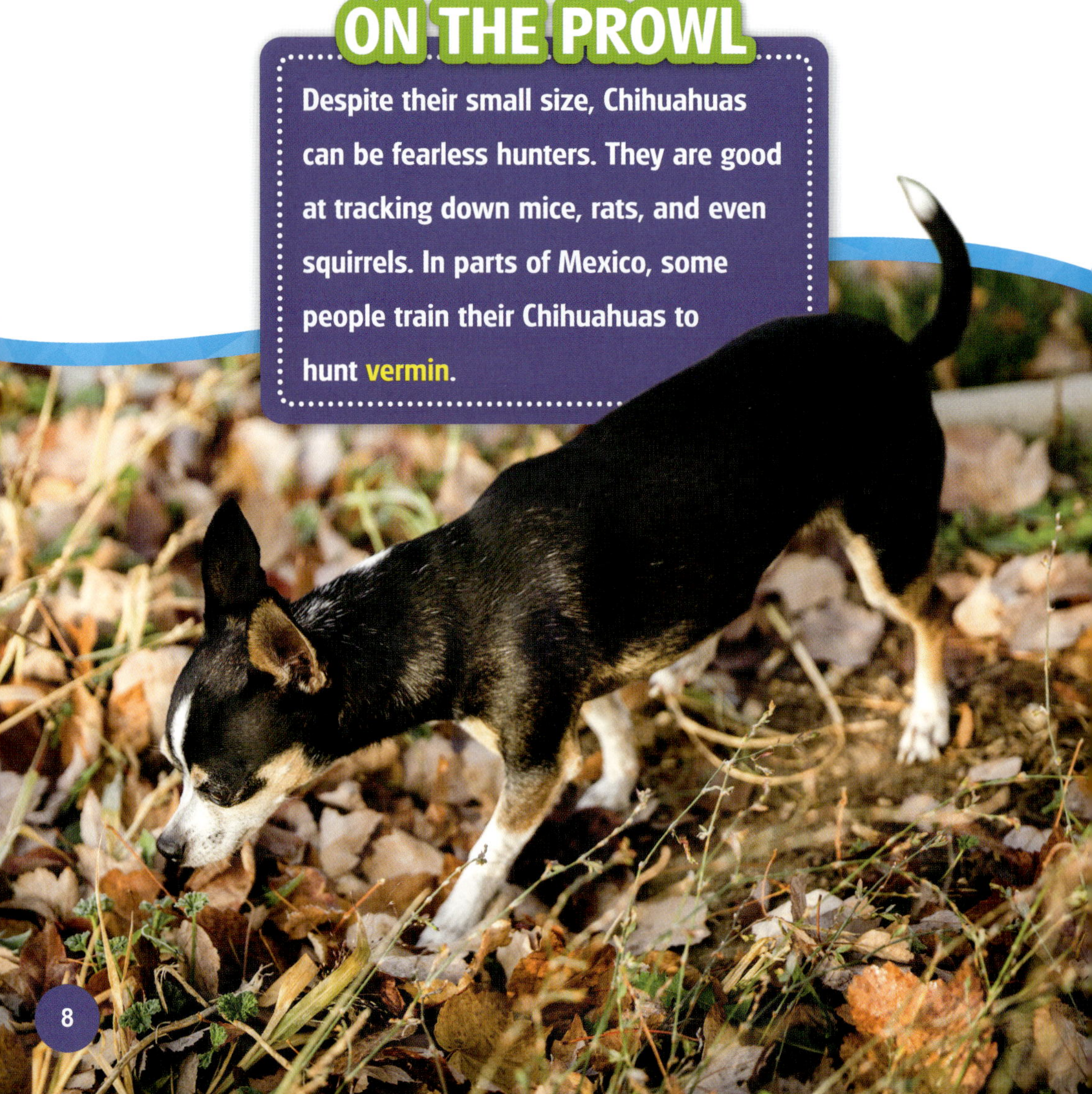

Pepper does a great job of keeping Ali company. They play together in the backyard for hours. She has a lot of energy. Ali is bigger, but he usually gets tired before Pepper does! Inside, she snuggles up in a blanket and sits on his lap. Pepper loves to **burrow** deep into pillows and blankets. Ali and his parents always check before they sit down!

WHERE CHIHUAHUAS COME FROM

UNITED STATES

Gulf of Mexico

MEXICO

Atlantic Ocean

Pacific Ocean

Mexico

FUN FACT

Chihuahuas tend to tremble. They do this when they are scared, nervous, or cold.

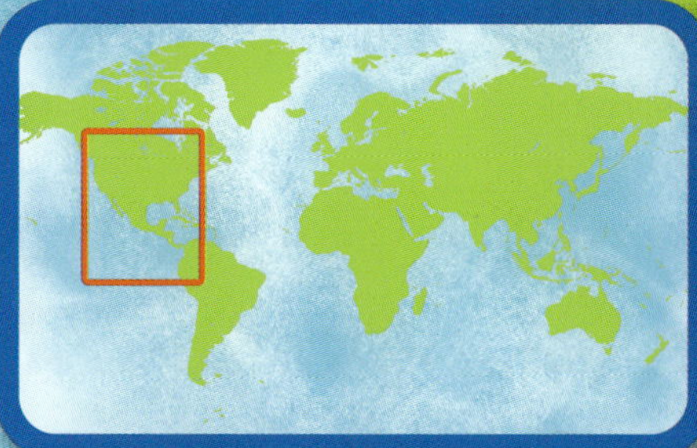

Chapter 2
Looking at a Chihuahua

It is easy to spot a Chihuahua. They have tiny bodies, large eyes, and pointy, bat-like ears. But there is also a lot of variety in the breed.

There are two main kinds of Chihuahuas. One kind is called smooth coat. They have very short hair. The other is long coat. That's what Pepper is.

Chis come in a huge range of colors and patterns. They can be white, black, red, brown, cream, silver, or fawn (light brown). They can be a solid color or a mix of colors. Pepper's coat is black and white. That is probably how she got her name.

FUN FACT
To compete in most dog shows, Chihuahuas must weigh 6 pounds (2.7 kg) or less.

Ali is glad Pepper is not too small. The **veterinarian** said extremely small dogs are usually not very healthy. Pepper is just right. Most Chihuahuas live about 14 to 18 years. Ali is looking forward to all of them!

THE

CHIHUAHUA

TAIL
Can curve over the back or be held upright

MALES AND FEMALES

HEIGHT*:
5-8 in. (12-20 cm)

WEIGHT:
5-6 lbs. (2.2-2.7 kg)

FUN FACT

Any longer hair on a Chi's back legs is called pants. On the neck, it's called a ruff.

The height of a dog is measured from the top of the shoulder, not from the top of the head.

HEAD
Apple-shaped
EARS
Upright
BACK
Level, not
sloping or
curved
FACE
Alert
expression
CHEST
Thickest
part of
body
FEET
Small, dainty

Chihuahuas can have two different head shapes. One looks like an apple. These Chis have round heads with short noses. The other is a deer head. They have flatter skulls and longer **muzzles**. Both are cute!

Their bodies can be **cobby** or long. A cobby body is smaller and more compact. The other body type is longer and thinner.

Many Chis have a soft spot, called a molera, on the top of their skulls. It is where the bones never grew together. If your Chi has a molera, make sure you protect her head from an injury.

Long body with deer head.

Cobby body with apple head.

Chapter 3

Meet a Chihuahua!

Chihuahuas are tiny, but they make up for it with big personalities! Pepper is alert, sassy, and curious. She always wants to know what is happening and how she can join in.

She likes to take walks. Ali puts her on a leash so she cannot get too far away. He doesn't want her to get hurt. If there are a lot of people around, he puts her in a carrier he wears on his chest. She pokes her head out of the top to look around. She likes watching everything from up high!

Chihuahuas like to be heard! A lot of them bark a lot. They are not big enough to be guard dogs who protect their owners from enemies. However, they make excellent watchdogs. If a stranger shows up, they will let you know!

Chihuahuas form very strong bonds with their people. They are loyal and want to protect their families. Sometimes Chihuahuas get jealous when other dogs or people come near. They may bark, growl, or bite.

Chihuahuas are known for their bravery. They do not realize how small they are. They will stand up to bigger, aggressive dogs.

Ali makes sure Pepper gets to meet lots of new people and pets. He teaches her to be friendly and get along with them. He does not want her to feel jealous. She does not need to worry about losing him. He will always love her the best!

SWEATER WEATHER

Chihuahuas are too small to hold their body heat well. Even 60°F (15.5°C) can feel chilly to them. If you take your Chi out in cold weather, keep the trips short—about 10 minutes. Ali got Pepper a coat to help keep her warm.

Chapter 4

Caring for a Chihuahua

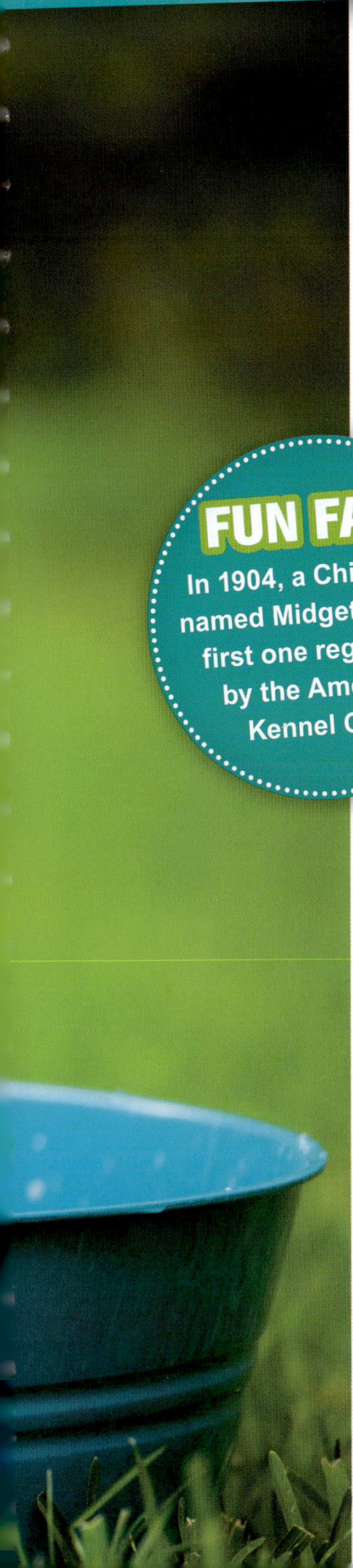

There isn't much to a Chihuahua, so **grooming** is pretty easy. Ali brushes Pepper's coat a couple of times a week. He uses a cotton ball to clean out her ears.

FUN FACT
In 1904, a Chihuahua named Midget was the first one registered by the American Kennel Club.

About once a month, he gives her a bath. He makes sure the water is not too hot or too cold. Chihuahuas are so small that their body temperature drops quickly in cold water. After Pepper's bath, Ali dries her thoroughly with a towel. Walking around with wet fur would also give her the chills.

Chis don't eat much, but they need to eat often. It is best to offer meals three times a day, plus small snacks in between. This helps them keep the right amount of **nutrients** in their bodies. Otherwise they may get tired or feel sick.

It's also important to keep their teeth clean. Chihuahuas have soft teeth that tend to **decay**. That can cause serious health problems. Ali brushes Pepper's teeth every night after dinner. He uses a toothpaste that's made just for dogs.

TREAT OR NOT TO TREAT?

Dogs love treats. Make sure they don't get too many! Healthy treats are a great way to train your dog. They can be a reward for doing something right. But too many treats can be unhealthy. Choose treats that are tasty and good for your dog.

At the end of the day, Pepper is still full of energy! But Ali is tired. He holds Pepper on his lap and pets her until she relaxes. Then he sets her in her dog bed. It is soft and snuggly, with plenty of blankets. Pepper digs in deep. Soon she is snoring away. Ali laughs. She can be pretty loud for such a small dog!

In the morning, they will play some more. Ali is glad Pepper picked him!

FUN FACT

In the late 1990s, a Chihuahua named Gidget became famous after being in ads for Taco Bell.

BEYOND THE BOOK

After reading the book, it's time to think about what you learned. Try the following exercises to jumpstart your ideas.

RESEARCH

FIND OUT MORE. There is so much more to find out about Chihuahuas. Visit the American Kennel Club's site to research Chihuahuas. Or look for a Chihuahua Club in your area. You can meet other people who love your favorite breed!

CREATE

TIME FOR ART. A baseball team in El Paso, Texas is named the Chihuahuas. Pick your favorite dog breed and design a new logo for a sports team named for that dog. What colors will you use? What sort of lettering? Will the dog look friendly or fierce? Look at other dog mascot logos for inspiration.

DISCOVER

LOTS OF BREEDS. This book is about your favorite dog breed. But there are hundreds more around the world. Visit the AKC site or those of other dog organizations. What other breeds can you discover? Which breeds are related to your favorite? What is the most interesting new breed you have discovered?

GROW

HELP OUT! Animal shelters can be great places to volunteer. Contact a shelter near you and find out if you can help. Or can your family donate food or gear to help rescue dogs? Find out why dogs end up in shelters. Is there anything you can do to help them find homes?

Visit www.ninjaresearcher.com/4385 to learn how to take your research skills and book report writing to the next level!

SEARCH LIKE A PRO
Learn about how to use search engines to find useful websites.

FACT OR FAKE?
Discover how you can tell a trusted website from an untrustworthy resource.

TEXT DETECTIVE
Explore how to zero in on the information you need most.

SHOW YOUR WORK
Research responsibly—learn how to cite sources.

WRITE

GET TO THE POINT
Learn how to express your main ideas.

PLAN OF ATTACK
Learn prewriting exercises and create an outline.

DOWNLOADABLE REPORT FORMS

Further Resources

BOOKS

Adelman, Beth. *Good Dog!: Dog Care for Kids.* Mankato, Minn.: Child's World: 2014.

Frank, Sarah. *Chihuahuas.* Minneapolis: Lerner Publications, 2019.

Gagne, Tammy. *Chihuahuas.* Minneapolis: Capstone Press, 2008.

WEBSITES

Factsurfer.com gives you a safe, fun way to find more information.

1. Go to www.factsurfer.com.
2. Enter "Chihuahuas" into the search box and click 🔍
3. Select your book cover to see a list of related websites.

Glossary

burrow: to dig deep and bury oneself.

cobby: a body type that is small and compact.

decay: to break down or go bad.

grooming: taking care of a dog's physical needs, such as brushing and bathing.

kennel: a small, closed space for an animal to live in.

molera: a small, soft spot on the skull.

muzzle: the part of the face that sticks out on an animal and includes the nose and mouth.

nutrients: things found in food that are necessary for good health.

vermin: small animals or insects that are considered pests.

veterinarian: a doctor for animals.

Index

PHOTO CREDITS

The images in this book are reproduced through the courtesy of: Alamy Stock: Florilegius 6. iStock: Cynoclub 4; nickpo 19; Hraun 21; Liliboas 26. Shutterstock: Shane Coat 8; Yashkin Ilya 9; Otsphoto 10; Miras Wonderland 12; anetapics 13; Susan Schmitz 14; Eric Isselee 16, 18; Di Soccio Massimo 17T; Robert Heber 17B; vmaze 20; BCFC 21; Vitaly Titov 22, 23.
Cover and page 1: MirasWonderland/iStock. Paw prints: Maximillian Laschon/Shutterstock.

About the Author

Diane Bailey has written more than 75 books for kids and teens, on subjects ranging from sports to science to history. She lives in Kansas, where she raised two sons, two Golden Retrievers, one hamster, one mouse, and 117 ants.